The Drunken Sisters

by Thornton Wilder

No one shall make any changes in this title for the purpose of production. No part of this book may be reproduced, stored in a retrieval system, or transmitted in any form, by any means, now known or yet to be invented, including mechanical, electronic, photocopying, recording, videotaping, or otherwise, without the prior written permission of the publisher. No one shall upload this title, or part of this title, to any social media websites.

MUSIC USE NOTE

Licensees are solely responsible for obtaining formal written permission from copyright owners to use copyrighted music in the performance of this play and are strongly cautioned to do so. If no such permission is obtained by the licensee, then the licensee must use only original music that the licensee owns and controls. Licensees are solely responsible and liable for all music clearances and shall indemnify the copyright owners of the play and their licensing agent, Samuel French, against any costs, expenses, losses and liabilities arising from the use of music by licensees. Please contact the appropriate music licensing authority in your territory for the rights to any incidental music.

IMPORTANT BILLING AND CREDIT REQUIREMENTS

All producers of *THE DRUNKEN SISTERS* must give credit to the author of the play in all programs distributed in connection with performances of the play, and in all instances in which the title of the play appears for the purposes of advertising, publicizing or otherwise exploiting the play and/ or a production. The name of the author must appear on a separate line on which no other name appears, immediately following the title and must appear in size of type not less than fifty percent of the size of the title type.

This play may be performed only in its entirety. No permission can be granted for cuttings, readings or any use of parts of the play for any purpose whatsoever without the express written permission of the Wilder Family LLC. Absolutely *no* changes can be made to the text.

FOREWORD TO WILDER'S
THE DRUNKEN SISTERS

THE SIN OF GLUTTONY

From the time he began dreaming up plays as a boy Thornton Wilder's vision of the theater transcended conventional boundaries, and to the end of his life his vision continually evolved and expanded. In 1956, he began work on what grew into an extravagantly ambitious project: two cycles of seven one-act plays based on the Deadly Sins and the Ages of Man. *The Drunken Sisters* represents "Gluttony" in Wilder's projected cycle on the Seven Deadly Sins. It is also the satyr play that followed *The Alcestiad*, Wilder's adaptation of the ancient Greek "Alcestis" story.

In what would prove to be his final dramatic works, Wilder sought not only to explore the theatrical possibilities inherent in the Sins and Ages, but (as he phrased it in his private journal on Christmas Day 1960) to "offer each play in the series as representing, also, a different mode of playwriting: Grand Guignol, Chekhov, Noh play, etc., etc." In short, he envisioned nothing less than a *tour de force* of dramatic theme and form encapsulated in the economy and intensity of the one-act play.

Wilder did not complete the challenge he set for himself, but he came close. The surviving work enriches his dramatic legacy and deserves to be remembered as more than a footnote to his lifelong conviction (written soon after *Our Town* opened on Broadway in 1938): "The theater offers to imaginative narration its highest possibilities."

THE SINS AND AGES THEN AND NOW

A brief overview of the history of these plays will help readers place them in Wilder's career as a dramatist. Two Sins, *Bernice* (Pride) and *The Wreck on the 5:25* (Sloth), premiered in English at a special event in Berlin in 1957 (with Wilder performing in *Bernice*). For reasons that have never been clear, for he enjoyed the experience and felt that plays did well, he withdrew them. That same year a third Sin, *The Drunken Sisters* (Gluttony), written as the satyr play for Wilder's full length drama, *The Alcestiad*, proved successful in its premiere on the stage of Zürich's fabled Schauspielhaus.

Five years passed before the continuation of his ambitious scheme appeared on a stage in the United States. In January 1962, two new Ages (*Infancy* and *Childhood*) and a new Sin, *Someone From Assisi* (Lust), opened at Circle in the Square, then located off-Broadway on Bleecker Street, to the reported largest pre-opening advanced sale in that stage's then 11- year history. Billed as "Plays for Bleecker Street," the show of ran for 349 performances.

Then silence. After "Plays for Bleecker Street" closed, no more Sins or Ages appeared. When Thornton Wilder died in 1975 the public record of his 14-play scheme contained only four plays – two Ages (*Infancy* and *Childhood*) and two Sins (Lust and Gluttony).

Today, eleven of Wilder's Sins and Ages are available for production: a completed cycle of the seven Deadly Sins and four of seven Ages of Man. The source of the seven "new" plays is no secret. The missing pieces were found in Thornton Wilder's archives at Yale[1]. From this source, starting in 1995, his literary executor and family released the two plays withdrawn in 1957, *Cement Hands* (Avarice), and four additional titles (*Youth*, *The Rivers Under the Earth* [Middle Age][2], *A Ringing of Doorbells* [Envy] and *In Shakespeare and the Bible* [Wrath]) recovered and completed by the actor, director and friend of Wilder's, F.J. O'Neil. (Mr. O'Neil's valuable notes on the origin of each of these missing links follow the text of each play.)

The public reception of Thornton Wilder's long lost and new plays was gratifying. *The Wreck on the 5:25* was selected as one of the Best American Short Plays of 1994-95. In 1997, the Centenary of the playwright's birth, Kevin Kline starred in a premiere reading in New York of *Cement Hands*, and the works recovered by Mr. O'Neil served as the centerpieces of Actors Theatre of Louisville's 13th Annual Brown-Forman Classics in Context Festival.   Finally, as the capstone to the Centenary celebration, TCG Press in 1997 published the 11 Sins and Ages in Volume I of *The Collected Short Plays of Thornton Wilder*.

---

[1] No additional one-acts remain to be discovered in Thornton Wilder's archives at Yale.

[2] We believe Wilder intended *The Rivers Under the Earth* to represent Middle Age.

Wilder never followed conventional theatrical practice. As a young writer in his "Classic One Act Plays" of 1931, he swept away scenery and played provocative games with time and place. In the Sins and Ages, his farewell as a playwright, he is no less adventurous by way of settings, techniques, stage-craft and themes. One artistic trend of the day especially "fired his imagination" where these plays are concerned: his passionate belief in the value of the arena stage. "The boxed set play," he wrote in 1961, "encourages the anecdote…The unencumbered stage encourages the truth in everyone." Wilder felt so strongly that audiences should be seated as close to the actors as possible that Samuel French, for several years, was only permitted to license these plays to companies agreeing to perform them on a three-sided thrust or arena stage.

***

As part of its celebration of Wilder's one-act plays, Samuel French and the Wilder family take great pleasure in issuing new acting editions for the Sins and Ages long in print and, for the first time, acting editions of the seven new Wilder works. We invite those performing or teaching these plays to visit www.thorntonwilder.com for additional information.

– Tappan Wilder,
Literary Executor for Thornton Wilder

CHARACTERS

CLOTHO – (pronounced KLO-tho) one of the *Three Fates*
LACHESIS – (pronounced lay-KEY-sis) one of the *Three Fates*
ATROPOS – (pronounced AA-tro-pos) one of the *Three Fates*
APOLLO – God of the Sun

SETTING

The time of Admetus, King of Thessaly.

(The only objects necessary for the setting of this play are a platform about two feet high on which the **THREE FATES** *are seated, and the bench beneath them. The bench is largely hidden by their voluminous draperies. They wear the masks of old women, touched by the grotesque but with vestiges of nobility. Seated from the players' Right to Left are* **CLOTHO** *with her spindle,* **LACHESIS** *with the bulk of the thread of life on her lap, and* **ATROPOS** *with her scissors. The designer should resort to every device in order to make them appear enormous and of wide knee-span. They rock back and forth as they work, passing the threads from right to left. The audience watches them for a time in silence, broken only by a faint humming from* **CLOTHO.**)

CLOTHO. What is it that goes first on four legs, then on two legs? Don't tell me! Don't tell me!

LACHESIS. *(bored)* You know it!

CLOTHO. Let me pretend that I don't know it.

ATROPOS. There are no new riddles. We know them all.

LACHESIS. How boring our life is without riddles! Clotho, make up a riddle.

CLOTHO. Be quiet, then, and give me a moment to think… What is it that…What is it that…?

(Enter **APOLLO,** *disguised. He wears a cone-shaped straw hat with a wide brim to conceal his face. Three flagons are hanging from a rope around his neck.)*

APOLLO. *(to the audience)* I am Apollo. In the disguise of a kitchen boy. I hate disguises. And I hate drunkenness – but see these bottles I have hanging around my neck? I hate lies and stratagems; but I've come here to do crookedly what even Allfather Zeus could not do without guile. These are the great sisters – the

Fates. Clotho weaves the threads of life; Lachesis measures the length of each; Atropos cuts them short. I have come to do a thing which has never been done before – to extend human life; to arrest the scissors of Atropos. Oh, to change the order of the universe.

ATROPOS. Sister! Your elbow! Do your work without striking me.

LACHESIS. I can't help it – this thread is s-o-o l-o-o-ong! Never have I had to reach so far.

CLOTHO. Long and gray and dirty! All those years a slave!

LACHESIS. So it is! *(to* **ATROPOS***)* Cut it, dear sister. **(ATROPOS** *cuts it – click!)* And now this one; cut this. It's a blue one – blue for bravery, blue and short.

ATROPOS. So easy to see!

(click)

LACHESIS. You almost cut that purple one, Atropos.

ATROPOS. This one? Purple for a king?

LACHESIS. Yes; watch what you're doing, dear. It's the life of Admetus, King of Thessaly.

APOLLO. *(aside)* Aie!

LACHESIS. I've marked it clearly. He's to die at sunset.

APOLLO. *(to the audience)* No! No!

LACHESIS. He's the favorite of Apollo, as was his father before him, and all that tiresome house of Thessaly. The queen Alcestis will be a widow tonight.

APOLLO. *(to the audience)* Alcestis! Alcestis! No!

LACHESIS. There'll be howling in Thessaly. There'll be rolling on the ground and tearing of garments…Not now dear; there's an hour yet.

APOLLO. *(aside)* To work! To work, Apollo the Crooked! *(He starts the motions of running furiously while remaining in one place, but stops suddenly and addresses the audience.)* Is there anyone here who does not know that old story – the reason why King Admetus and his queen Alcestis are dear to me? *(He sits on the ground and continues talking with raised forefinger.)* Was it ten years ago? I am little concerned with time. I am the god of the sun; it is always light where I am. Perhaps ten years ago. My father and the father of us all was filled up with anger against me. What had I done? *(He moves his finger hack and forth.)* Do not ask that now; let it be forgotten…He laid upon me a punishment. He ordered that I should descend to earth and live for a year among men – *I*, as a man among men, as a servant. Half hidden, known and not known, I chose to be a herdsman of King Admetus of Thessaly. I lived the life of a man, as close to them as I am to you now, as close to the just and to the unjust. Each day the King gave orders to the other herdsmen and myself; each day the Queen gave thought to what went well or ill with us and our families. I came to love King Admetus and Queen Alcestis and through them I came to love all men. And now Admetus must die. *(rising)* No! I have laid my plans. I shall prevent it. To work. To work, Apollo the Crooked. *(He again starts the motions of running furiously while remaining in one place. He complains noisily.)* Oh, my back! Aie, aie. They beat me, but worst of all they've made me late. I'll be beaten again.

LACHESIS. Who's the sniveler?

APOLLO. Don't stop me now. I haven't a moment to talk. I'm late already. Besides, my errand's a terrible secret. I can't say a word.

ATROPOS. Throw your yarn around him, Lachesis. What's the fool doing with a secret? It's we who have all the secrets.

(The threads in the laps of the Sisters are invisible to the audience. LACHESIS now rises and swings her hands three times in wide circles above her head as though she were about to fling a lasso, then hurls the noose across the stage. APOLLO makes the gesture of being caught. With each strong pull by LACHESIS, APOLLO is dragged nearer to her. During the following speeches LACHESIS lifts her end of the strands high in the air, alternately pulling APOLLO up, almost strangling him, and flinging him again to the ground.)

APOLLO. Ladies, beautiful ladies, let me go. If I'm late all Olympus will be in an uproar. Aphrodite will be mad with fear – but oh, already I've said too much. My orders were to come immediately, and to say nothing especially not to women. The thing's of no interest to men. Dear ladies, let me go.

ATROPOS. Pull on your yarn, sister.

APOLLO. You're choking me. You're squeezing me to death.

LACHESIS. *(forcefully)* Stop your whining and tell your secret at once.

APOLLO. I can't. I dare not.

ATROPOS. Pull harder, sister. Boy, speak or strangle.

(She makes the gesture of choking him.)

APOLLO. Ow! Ow! – Wait! I'll tell the half of it, if you let me go.

ATROPOS. Tell the whole or we'll hang you up in the air in that noose.

APOLLO. I'll tell, I'll tell. But – *(He looks about him fearfully.)* – promise me! Swear by the Styx that you'll not tell anyone, and swear by Lethe that you'll forget it.

LACHESIS. We have only one oath – by Acheron. And we never swear it – least of all to a sniveling slave. Tell us what you know, or you'll be by all three rivers in a minute.

APOLLO. I tremble at what I am about to say. I…ssh…I carry…here…in these bottles… Oh, ladies, let me go. Let me go.

CLOTHO & ATROPOS. Pull, sister.

APOLLO. No! No! I'll tell you. I am carrying the wine for… for Aphrodite. Once every ten days she renews her beauty…by…drinking this.

ATROPOS. Liar! Fool! She has nectar and ambrosia, as they all have.

APOLLO. *(confidentially)* But is she not the fairest?… It is the love gift of Hephaistos; from the vineyards of Dionysos;

from grapes ripened under the eye of Apollo – of Apollo who tells no lies.

SISTERS. *(confidentially to one another in blissful anticipation)* Sisters!

ATROPOS. *(like sugar)* Pass the bottles up, dear boy.

APOLLO. *(in terror)* Not that! Ladies! It is enough that I have told you the secret! Not that!

ATROPOS. Surely, Lachesis, you can find on your lap the thread of this worthless slave – a yellow one destined for a long life?

APOLLO. *(falling on his knees)* Spare me!

ATROPOS. *(to **LACHESIS**)* Look, that's it – the sallow one, with the tangle in it of dishonesty, and the stiffness of obstinacy, and the ravel – ravel of stupidity. Pass it over to me, dear.

APOLLO. *(his forehead touching the floor)* Oh, that I had never been born!

LACHESIS. *(to **ATROPOS**)* This is it. *(with a sigh)* I'd planned to give him five score.

APOLLO. *(rising and extending the bottles, sobbing)* Here, take them! I'll be killed anyway. Aphrodite will kill me. My life's over.

ATROPOS. *(strongly, as the **SISTERS** take the bottles)* Not one more word out of you. Put your hand on your mouth. We're tired of listening to you.

*(**APOLLO**, released of the noose, flings himself facedown upon the ground, his shoulders heaving. The **SISTERS** put the flagons to their lips. They drink and moan with pleasure.)*

LACHESIS. Sisters!

ATROPOS. Sisters!

CLOTHO. Sisters!

LACHESIS. Sister, how do I look?

ATROPOS. Oh, I could eat you. And I?

CLOTHO. Sister, how do I look?

LACHESIS. Beautiful! Beautiful! And I?

ATROPOS. And not a mirror on all the mountain, or a bit of still water, to tell us which of us is the fairest.

LACHESIS. *(dreamily, passing her hand over her face)* I feel like…I feel as I did when Kronos followed me about, trying to catch me in a dark corner.

ATROPOS. Poseidon was beside himself – dashing across the plains trying to engulf me.

CLOTHO. My own father – who can blame him? – began to forget himself.

ATROPOS. *(whispering)* This is not such a worthless fellow, after all. And he's not bad-looking. *(to* CLOTHO*)* Ask him what he sees.

LACHESIS. Ask him which of us is the fairest.

CLOTHO. Boy! Boy! You bay meek. I mean, you…you may thpeak. Thpeak to him, Lakethith; I've lotht my tongue.

LACHESIS. Boy, look at us well! You may tell us which is the fairest.

(Each of the SISTERS *is drunk in a different way.* CLOTHO *becomes a little girl.* LACHESIS *arrogant and quarrelsome,* ATROPOS *tearful.)*

CLOTHO. Of courth, I'm the yougeth. I've always been a darling. Everybody saith – simply everybody saith – Darling Clotho. Thweet Clotho.

LACHESIS. *(striking her)* Yes, youngest and silliest – and vulgarest. I don't care who the fool says is fairest. I wouldn't expect to find taste in a kitchen boy. Who cares for the admiration of the marketplace?

ATROPOS. No one has ever been just to me. People say that I'm cruel. I'm not cruel. I've the tenderest heart in the world. I spend my life doing my duty, and what do I get for it? – ingratitude!

(They start talking simultaneously. LACHESIS *is the loudest.)*

LACHESIS. Go find a judge who knows beauty when he sees it. Not a shallow pettiness, like you, Clotho, nor a bitter face like yours, Atropos, but soul. Soul. Spirit. Majesty. Dignity. Soul.

CLOTHO. Of courth, I'm *little.* I've always been little. When I path'd everybody said: mi-mi-mi-mi; come here, you little darling. Mi-mi-mi-mi, you little darling.

ATROPOS. Hidden away on this mountain. One injustice after another. And what do I get for it? – ingratitude. the tenderest heart in the world – that's what I have.

LACHESIS. *(silencing them)* Hold your tongues, geese, and let's put the question to the young man. Boy, get up. Don't be afraid. Tell us: in your opinion, which of us is the fairest?

(**APOLLO** *has remained face downward on the ground. He now rises and gazes at the* **SISTERS**. *He acts as if blinded he cowers and uncovers his eyes, gazing first at one and then at another.)*

APOLLO. What have I done? This splendor! What have I done? You – and you – and you! Kill me if you will, but I cannot say which one is the fairest. *(falling on his knees)* Oh, ladies – if so much beauty has not made you cruel, let me now go and hide myself. Aphrodite will hear of this. Let me escape to Crete and take up my old work.

ATROPOS. What was your former work, dear boy?

APOLLO. I helped my father in the marketplace; I was a teller of stories and riddles.

(The **SISTERS** *are transfixed. Then almost with a scream.)*

SISTERS. What's that? What's that you said?

APOLLO. A teller of stories and riddles. Do the beautiful ladies enjoy riddles?

SISTERS. *(rocking from side to side and slapping one another)* Sisters, do we enjoy riddles?

ATROPOS. Oh, he would only know the *old* ones. Puh! The blind horse...the big toe...

LACHESIS. The cloud…the eyelashes of Hera…

CLOTHO. *(harping on one string)* What is it that first goes on four legs…?

ATROPOS. The porpoise…Etna…

APOLLO. Everyone knows those! I have some new ones –

SISTERS. *(again, a scream)* New ones!

APOLLO. *(slowly)* What is it that is necessary to –

(He pauses. The SISTERS *are riveted.)*

LACHESIS. Go on, boy, go on. What is it that is necessary to –

APOLLO. But – I only play for forfeits. See! If I lose…

CLOTHO. If you looth, you mutht tell uth which one ith the faireth.

APOLLO. No! No! I dare not!

LACHESIS. *(sharply)* Yes!

APOLLO. And if I win?

ATROPOS. Win? Idiot! Stupid! Slave! No one has ever won from us.

APOLLO. But if I win?

LACHESIS. He doesn't know who we are!

APOLLO. But if I win?

CLOTHO. The fool talkth of winning!

APOLLO. If I win, you must grant me one wish. One wish, any wish.

LACHESIS. Yes, yes. Oh, what a tedious fellow! Go on with your riddle. What is it that is necessary to –

APOLLO. Swear by Acheron!

CLOTHO & LACHESIS. We swear! By Acheron! By Acheron!

APOLLO. *(to* ATROPOS*)* You, too.

ATROPOS. *(after a moment's brooding resistance, loudly)* By Acheron!

APOLLO. Then: ready?

LACHESIS. Wait! One moment. *(leaning toward* ATROPOS, *confidentially)* The sun is near setting. Do not forget the thread of Ad – You know, the thread of Ad –

ATROPOS. What? What Ad? What are you whispering about, silly?

LACHESIS. *(somewhat louder)* Not to forget the thread of Admetus, King of Thessaly. At sundown. Have you lost your shears, Atropos?

ATROPOS. Oh, stop your buzzing and fussing and tend to your own business. Of course I haven't lost my shears. Go on with your riddle, boy!

APOLLO. So! I'll give you as much time as it takes to recite the names of the Muses and their mother.

LACHESIS. Hm! Nine and one. Well, begin!

APOLLO. What is it that is necessary to every life – and that can save only one?

> *(The* **SISTERS** *rock back and forth with closed eyes, mumbling the words of the riddle. Suddenly* **APOLLO** *starts singing his invocation to the Muses.)*

Mnemosyne, mother of the nine;

Polyhymnia, incense of the gods –

LACHESIS. *(shrieks)* Don't sing! Unfair! How can we think?

CLOTHO. Stop your ears, sister.

ATROPOS. Unfair! *(murmuring)* What is it that can save every life –

> *(They put their fingers in their ears.)*

APOLLO. Erato, voice of love;

Euterpe, help me now.

Calliope, thief of our souls;

Urania, clothed of the stars;

Clio of the backward glances;

Euterpe, help me now.

Terpsichore of the beautiful ankles;

Thalia of long laughter;

Melpomene, dreaded and welcome;

Euterpe, help me now.

> *(then in a loud voice)* Forfeit! Forfeit!

(**CLOTHO** *and* **ATROPOS** *bury their faces in* **LACHESIS**'*s neck, moaning.*)

LACHESIS. *(in a dying voice)* What is the answer?

APOLLO. *(flinging away his hat, triumphantly)* Myself! Apollo the sun.

SISTERS. Apollo! You?

LACHESIS. *(savagely)* Pah! What life can you save?

APOLLO. My forfeit! One wish! One life! That life of Admetus, King of Thessaly.

(*A horrified clamor arises from the* **SISTERS.**)

SISTERS. Fraud! Impossible! Not to be thought of!

APOLLO. By Acheron.

SISTERS. Against all law. Zeus will judge. Fraud.

APOLLO. *(warning)* By Acheron.

SISTERS. Zeus! We will go to Zeus about it. He will decide.

APOLLO. Zeus swears by Acheron and keeps his oath. *(sudden silence)*

ATROPOS. *(decisive but ominous)* You will have your wish – the life of King Admetus. But –

APOLLO. *(triumphantly)* I shall have the life of Admetus!

SISTERS. But –

APOLLO. I shall have the life of Admetus! What is your but?

ATROPOS. Someone else must die in his stead.

APOLLO. *(lightly)* Oh – choose some slave. Some gray and greasy thread on your lap, divine Lachesis.

LACHESIS. *(outraged)* What? You ask me to take a life?

ATROPOS. You ask us to murder?

CLOTHO. Apollo thinks that we are criminals?

APOLLO. *(beginning to be fearful)* Then, great sisters, how is this to be done?

LACHESIS. Me – an assassin? *(she spreads her arms wide and says solemnly)* Over my left hand is Chance; over my right hand is Necessity.

APOLLO. Then, gracious sisters, how will this be done?

LACHESIS. Someone must *give* his life for Admetus – of free choice and will. Over such deaths we have no control. Neither Chance nor Necessity rules the free offering of the will. Someone must choose to die in the place of Admetus, King of Thessaly.

APOLLO. *(covering his face with his hands)* No! No! I see it all! *(with a loud cry)* Alcestis! Alcestis! *(And he runs stumbling from the scene.)*

End of Play

THORNTON WILDER (1897-1975) was an accomplished novelist and playwright whose works explore the connection between the commonplace and the cosmic dimensions of human experience. He won three Pulitzer Prizes: for his novel *The Bridge of San Luis Rey*, and two plays, *Our Town* and *The Skin of Our Teeth*. Wilder's farce, *The Matchmaker*, was adapted as the musical *Hello, Dolly!* He also enjoyed enormous success as a translator, adaptor, actor, librettist and lecturer/teacher. Wilder's many honors include the Gold Medal for Fiction from the American Academy of Arts and Letters and the Presidential Medal of Freedom. Penelope Niven's definitive biography, *Thornton Wilder: A Life*, was published in October 2012. For more information, please visit www.thorntonwilder.com.

Also by
Thornton Wilder...

The Alcestiad

The Beaux' Stratagem (with Ken Ludwig)

The Matchmaker

Our Town

The Skin of Our Teeth

Thornton Wilder One Act Series: The Ages of Man

Infancy

Childhood

Youth

The Rivers Under the Earth

Thornton Wilder One Act Series: Wilder's Classic One Acts

The Long Christmas Dinner

Queens of France

Pullman Car Hiawatha

Love and How to Cure It

Such Things Only Happen in Books

The Happy Journey to Trenton and Camden

Thornton Wilder One Act Series: The Seven Deadly Sins

The Drunken Sisters

Bernice

The Wreck on the 5:25

A Ringing of Doorbells

In Shakespeare and the Bible

Someone From Assisi

Cement Hands

Please visit our website **samuelfrench.com** for complete descriptions and licensing information.

www.ingramcontent.com/pod-product-compliance
Lightning Source LLC
Chambersburg PA
CBHW070424120726
47909CB00005B/1782